CHAPTER ONE

Dylan

STOP.

Just keep it together.

My grizzly lets out a low ferocious growl and three of my brothers glance nervously at me.

Not now. Please, not now.

My asshole grizzly is picking the worst time to have a tantrum. It's like living with a psychotic two-year-old who hasn't learned boundaries yet.

I can feel him pacing around inside, huffing angrily and snarling at the smell of love in the air.

This time, even the groom who is my youngest brother, Nathan, turns around. It's the middle of his wedding ceremony and he looks worried that his older brother won't be able to keep his insane grizzly bear in check.

It's a valid concern. I've been having a lot of trouble lately.

It started when my older brother Caleb found his mate. My grizzly started getting more and more upset that we didn't have our mate and he began taking it out on me.

Keeping me up all night by thrashing around inside and trying to claw his way out at the worst possible times. He was always a pain in the ass—more savage and violent than all four of my brothers' bears combined—but lately, he's moving toward full-on feral and I don't know how to stop it.

Caleb finding his mate was bad, but when my younger brothers, Scott and Lionel, found their mates too, he got worse. He actually burst out of my body when we met Lionel's mate, Aubrey, and ran into the woods, snarling like a rabid beast. I couldn't pull him in for four days.

When Nathan found his mate, Candice, at only twenty-two years-old, a full ten years younger than me, my enraged bear kept me up for three straight nights and days.

"It is now time for the vows," the minister says.

My whole body is flexed in this tuxedo as I struggle to hold my barbaric grizzly back. I'm sweating. My breaths are all harsh and ragged. This is not a good look.

I force out a smile to the crowd. Some of them are looking back at me, probably wondering if I'm having a stroke.

Nathan and Candice are mates, so this wedding is pretty useless. What's more of a connection, more of a bond, more of a commitment than being a fated mate?

But still, Candice is human, so it was important to her and her family. Nathan is willing to do anything for her, so he went along with it all.

I should have sat this one out. I should have known.

"From the second I met you," Candice says to her mate

AUCTIONED TO THE GRIZZLY SHIFTER

HIGHEST BIDDER

OLIVIA T. TURNER

www.OliviaTTurner.com

Edited by Picky Cat Editing
Cover Design by Cormar Covers

To Natalie,
Who likes chests as hairy as they get.

with a look of pure devotion in her eyes, "I knew you were the one."

My bear starts boiling at the words. He lets out a nasty growl and charges forward. I grunt as I flex my whole body, trying desperately to hold him in.

The humans can't hear his noises, but the shifters can. My brothers turn to me with worried glances. My family in the crowd is on the edge of their seats, knowing what my maniac of a bear is capable of.

I can't let Nathan and Candice down. I *won't.*

Fuck off! I growl back.

My bear takes this as a challenge and lunges forward, trying to pull me in as he claws his way out. I stumble back as I squeeze my eyes shut, gritting my teeth as I force him down. It's like trying to stop a tsunami. It's like trying to push down an earthquake.

We're not doing this fucking shit here! Fuck. Off.

He snarls and bounds forward again in a brutal charge. I nearly drop to my knee as I struggle to hold him in. I grab my tie and yank it loose so I can fucking breathe. My head is pounding. My pulse is racing. I hate this fucking bear.

He's always been a fucker. An untamed, wild predator that I had to share this body with. But this—ruining my brother's wedding—is a new low. Even for him.

I can feel my body swelling, my skin tightening as he ruthlessly tries to break free. My gums are on fire as his teeth slowly push out, replacing my own.

Just before I feel the long brown fur sprouting out of my skin, I get a handle on him and shove him back down to the dark depths inside me.

When I open my eyes and come back to reality, I'm breathing heavily and hunched over. Scott and Lionel are holding my arms. Everyone is looking at me now—the bride, the groom, the minister, and every one of the guests.

"Sorry," I spit out. "I'm feeling a little faint."

I catch Nathan's eye. "Dude," he whispers. "Are you okay?"

I shake my head, straighten my tuxedo jacket, and excuse myself.

Everyone's eyes are on me as I hurry away from the ceremony. I can feel each one burning into my back.

Once I'm around the building, out of view from the gawking crowd, I run my hand through my brown hair and curse out my bear for ruining one more thing in my life.

"One hour," I hiss. "You couldn't let me have one fucking hour?"

My grizzly snarls back, furious that I'm standing here and taking a minute for myself. He wants me out there every single second of every day searching endlessly for my mate.

I've looked. I've searched for fifteen fucking years and I still haven't found her.

I'm always trying to calm my bear down, but the reality is, I'm pissed too. At the universe, at myself, at fate. Where the fuck is she? What the fuck do I have to do?

All of my brothers have their mates and I got nothing. It's not fair. It's not fucking fair.

I can barely handle it anymore.

I'm so caught up in my own shit that I don't notice my uncle Andrew until he's limping right up to me. He's an old grizzled grizzly bear shifter and probably the only one who understands me. He's got a raving furry lunatic for a bear too.

"When was the last time you let him out?"

Let him out. That's a laugh. Half of the time, he comes bursting out of me whenever he wants. If I let him out the fucker might not let me back in for days.

"He was out last week."

My uncle sighs as he looks at me. "I always hoped you weren't going to be the last one to find your mate. I knew it would have been especially hard on your bear."

"Well, you were right," I say as I drop my shoulders in defeat. "I ruined Nathan's wedding."

"No," he says as he exhales long and hard. "All the shifters back there understand."

"And the humans?"

He shrugs. "They have a bear shifter in their family now. Will probably have some shifter cubs soon. It's about time they learn what we're about."

I close my eyes and drop my head. "They're probably going to be terrified of us now. It's not the impression of shifters I wanted to make."

"At least you didn't phase," he says as he pulls out a pack of smokes and taps one out. "That would have been ugly."

He laughs as he lights his cigarette. I just stare at him.

The smell of the smoke makes my bear livid and he charges forward with a new onslaught of aggression. I stumble back against the brick wall as I struggle to hold him down. *Fuck, you,* I snarl as I pound him down. He's getting stronger. Faster. I've never seen him like this. It's always been bad, but this is getting scary. I'm not sure if I'll be able to control him for much longer. Every day it gets worse.

He slices and claws at me as I force him down. It takes everything out of me and when he's finally back in, huffing and puffing angrily, I drop to my knee, exhausted and ready to throw in the towel.

"Your jacket," my uncle points out.

"Shit."

He got so close to the surface that my arms swelled up and the seams of my tuxedo jacket tore over my triceps. Should have gotten the insurance on the rental. I wonder how much this will set me back.

"It's not good," my uncle says as he calmly smokes his cigarette. "I can smell him. He's close to being feral."

Fuck. I wasn't sure if it was that bad, but now that I know, it's not a total surprise.

"I can tell you're barely hanging on. How long has it been this bad?"

"A couple of weeks," I say, still breathless from the fierce internal battle. "Since Nathan found his mate, but even before that it was bad. But not this bad."

"He's close to turning," he says with sad eyes. "If you lose control of that animal, your brothers are going to have a tough decision on their hands."

"I won't let it get to that," I say in a firm voice, but my trembling hands aren't so sure.

He grunts as he looks me over. "It's already getting dangerously close to that and you're not looking too in control."

I look at my torn jacket with the crisp white dress shirt underneath. At least that didn't tear. I made sure to get the synthetic stretchy kind.

"I think you're right," I say as a feeling of defeat takes over. "I'll kill myself before I let him go feral."

"Finding your mate will reverse the worst of it. Finding her will bring him back in control. You have to find her before he goes to the dark side."

I throw my hands in the air and grit my teeth. "I know that. But where the fuck is she?"

He frowns as he watches me. "She can be around the corner ready to pop into your life or she could be on the other side of the planet wandering around in Australia."

Just the thought of her out there in the world without my protective eyes on her makes me and my bear crazy. He snarls low. I agree with him on that one.

"So, how does that help me?"

"There's another way," my uncle says.

"There is?"

"Your bear is desperate to mate," he says with a nod. "But if he can't have his fated mate, you can keep your bear busy with someone else."

"Out of the question," I practically snarl.

He puts his hand up, like he wants me to hear him out, but I can't. I won't. I don't want someone else. I only want her.

I'd rather slit my throat than be unfaithful to my girl, to my mate.

"You don't have much of a choice," my uncle says, raising his voice. "You're going to get a bullet in the head if you're not careful. You can still have your mate when she comes, but in the meantime... nothing wrong with keeping your bear busy."

I can feel my jaw clenching. I don't like this at all. Even talking about it is making me tight and edgy all over.

"Your bear is a width of fur away from going full-on feral," my uncle points out. "And then what good are you going to be for your mate when she arrives? You'll be dead. If your brothers don't put a bullet in your head, then I will. We can't have a feral bear running around town, terrorizing these nice folks. Dylan, listen to reason. This may be your last chance."

Oh, fuck. I squeeze my eyes shut. I can't… How the hell has it come to this?

"The woman who runs this, Coco St. James… She's an old friend of mine. She'll find someone to keep your bear calm."

He hands me a business card.

I hate myself for taking it.

Breeding Bidders Auction House.

"You can't be serious," I say in a trembling voice as my bear's rage amps back up. He likes this topic of conversation even less than I do. "An auction? For what? Women?"

"Just keep an open mind," he says as my bear comes charging forward, thrashing and mauling his way out. "And keep your bear away from the reception for your brother's sake."

This time, I have no hope to hold him in. He explodes out of me in a burst of long brown fur, cruel black claws, and nasty white teeth. He roars at my uncle who calmly inhales his cigarette while watching through a cloud of smoke.

"Think about it, Dylan," he says, knowing I can hear him from deep down in here. I'm in a dark lonely place inside my bear. A place that I might never leave if my grizzly turns feral. "It's for your own good."

Into the woods, I beg the beast, pulling him away from the wedding. He wants to go investigate the ceremony, but he's not totally feral yet. I still have some pull on the monster.

He huffs out a frustrated breath, tramples over my torn tuxedo rental, and then sprints into the forest in the distance.

I can feel his power growing. It feels like every time I phase, he gets stronger.

There's no way I can pull him back in like this. It might be days before he lets me back out.

He slams his shoulder into a tree as he disappears into the forest, about to terrorize the local wildlife for a few hours.

I hate to admit it, but my uncle might be right.

If I don't keep this wild bear busy with someone soon, he'll turn feral for good.

And then I'll be getting a bullet in my head.

CHAPTER TWO

Lucy

REMEMBER WHEN STICKERS WERE FUN?

I want to go back to that time. Lighting up with joy inside when my teacher would stick a star on my shirt for getting the right answer. Stickers in loot bags and in Christmas stockings. I couldn't get enough of them.

Now? Not so much.

This sticker on my door is not filling me with joy. It's filling me with dread.

This bright yellow sticker has *Eviction* written across it in big black letters and is currently sticking my door to the doorframe. I look at the keys in my hand as I try not to be sick all over my welcome mat that I bought for fifty cents at a thrift store shortly after moving in.

"Please work," I whisper as I bring my key up to the shiny brass lock that I can already tell is brand-new. My key doesn't even slide in all the way. It stops halfway as my stomach sinks.

Ziggy barks at me through the door and my breath catches in my chest. They didn't even take him out before they sealed the place shut?

"It's okay, buddy," I quietly say through the door. "Just be quiet, okay? I'll come get you."

Shit. What the hell am I going to do?

My mind races through possibilities, but I'm not coming up with any good ones. I'm all alone in the city and have no money to fall back on. No couches to crash on. No friends who can help out.

It's been two years since I made my fresh start here in Montana and I'm embarrassed to say that I haven't made any close friends. I arrived right when the pandemic hit and it's pretty hard to make friends when you don't leave your place.

I fell into debt, but I've been trying to claw my way out of it with a shitty job in a warehouse where everyone is too busy running around like jackals at dinnertime to become friends.

"Miss West," a deep voice says from behind me. I spin around with a gasp.

"Mr. Reed," I say with my voice racing. "What is this? Changed locks? Eviction notice? I paid my rent last month. Didn't you get it?"

"I got it," he says with a stern look. "Late as usual."

His big gray eyebrows always come together when he looks at me with disapproval. "But you're not allowed dogs in the building. It's in your lease."

"But... I... Mrs. Patterson has a dog!"

"There's an exception for her. She was living here before the rules changed."

"Can't you make an exception for me?" I beg. "I always pay my rent. I'm quiet. I have no friends! He's a good dog!"

"Out of the question," he says with a frown. "Absolutely no dogs on the premises. I'm allergic and I hate them."

"But I keep him inside. I take the back stairs instead of the elevator. He doesn't make any noise! *Please.*"

Of course Ziggy chooses now to start barking up a storm.

Shut up, dude. Seriously!

Mr. Reed grumbles. "You're out."

"But you can't just kick me out on the street! You have to give me a warning or some time to figure something out. There's got to be laws about that!"

"There is," he says curtly. "And I followed them. I issued you three warnings."

"What?! When?!"

"I called the phone number on your lease and left three voicemails as required by law."

I yank my phone out of my purse in a panic. I never got a—*shit.*

"Remember I was originally subletting from that blonde girl Kindrie for the last two months of her lease? I still didn't have a phone when I took over the lease, so I think I might have left her number on it."

He shrugs. "That's fraud."

"It was just an innocent mistake!" I nearly scream. "You can't evict me! I have nowhere else to go."

I'm trying really hard not to cry here. Mr. Reed doesn't seem moved at all. I guess you have to have a heart of stone to be a landlord in this day and age. I'm sure I'm not the first person to cry at his feet with a sob story.

"Are you going to get rid of your dog?" he asks.

My mouth goes dry as I stare at him in panic. "I..."

He grunts knowingly. "Well then. Don't try to access the apartment again. You are officially evicted."

"But what about my stuff? What about my dog?"

"Your stuff will be placed on the grass out front tomorrow morning when my sons come to empty the apartment."

"And my dog? Are you just going to throw him out too?"

"I was going to bring him to the pound, but if you want to take him now that would save me a trip."

He's looking at me like it's even a question. "Yes!" I say. "Obviously, I'll take him."

I step back as he cuts the sticker with his key and then opens the door. Ziggy bounds out of the apartment and nearly tackles me to the ground.

My eyes water as I wrap my arms around his white furry body, breathing in his comforting smell.

"Can I just get—"

He slams the door closed and locks it once again. "Tomorrow morning."

"But I have nothing to feed him! I don't even have a change of clothes."

"Tomorrow morning," he says in a callous tone. "Now please leave the premises or I'll call the police to escort you off."

"But..."

There's no use in arguing with him. He's a heartless ass.

I grab Ziggy's collar since I wasn't even allowed to grab his leash, and leave while trying to hold it together.

My dad is on the other side of the country and I

haven't talked to him in over a year. Not since I found out that he had a new girlfriend only five days after the funeral. I'm not about to break the silence now by calling and asking him for money.

This is not good.

Ziggy is way too excited—why can't dogs ever read the freaking room?—and is pulling like crazy, expecting a walk.

I drag him to my old shitty car and put him in the back. He starts whimpering and pacing around nervously, expecting a visit to the vet.

"Get used to it," I say as I sit in the driver's seat and stare forward with dead eyes. "We'll be here for a while."

I'm up all night with my dog who refuses to settle, the hot summer air, and the fear of falling asleep with the car windows down. I finally fall asleep when I'm supposed to be awake.

I jerk up with a gasp and look at my dying phone to see the time. *Shit, it's ten o'clock!*

I quickly turn the car on and speed over to my old apartment building. "No!"

All of my stuff is on the grass, well, it was on the grass. The whole neighborhood has picked through everything I own and left only a few worthless items. I explode out of the car and rush over to look—a couch pillow, the top half of my blender, a pink sock, a few old romance novels I bought at a garage sale last summer.

Crap. They took everything.

I don't even bother taking what's left. I drop my head

as tears pour down my cheeks and stumble back to my car.

I have to call in sick. I can't go to work all day and leave Ziggy in the car. Not in this heat.

Even if I could go to work, my shift started half an hour ago and it's a twenty-minute drive.

I dial my boss with my heart hammering away in my chest.

"Stacy!" I say, trying to make my voice sound as desperate as I feel. "I'm sorry I'm not there."

"What time will you be here?"

"I... That's the thing... I... can't make it in today."

Silence except for her annoyed breathing.

"There's been an emergency!"

"Do you have a doctor's note?"

"No, but I—"

"You can't be absent without a doctor's note unless it's been pre-scheduled."

"Right, but something happened!"

"I'm listening."

"I got evicted! They threw out all of my stuff and I lost everything."

"Mm hm," she mumbles, not even caring a bit. *"That's not a suitable reason, Lucy. You were late twice this month alone—"*

"Because my car broke down! I told you that!"

"—and this absence makes three. You are officially terminated from Johnson-Stack Warehouse Inc. You can pick up your paycheck on Thursday."

"But—"

She hangs up.

FUCK!!!

I slam my hand on the steering wheel and scream until tears come pouring out.

Ziggy jumps into the front seat and licks my salty cheeks. This is so bad. So freaking bad.

I bury my face into his fur and sob until even he gets tired of me and jumps into the backseat to lie down.

I'm so screwed.

It's been four days of living in my car while trying to find a new apartment that doesn't require any money down and trying to find a new job that doesn't need a printed resume. It's not going well.

When Mr. Reed dumped all of my stuff on the grass, someone took my book of passwords and used it to sign into my online bank. All of my money is gone and they maxed out my credit card. Who knows what else they're doing with it? I don't even want to think about any loans they're taking out under my name or new credit cards they're applying for.

This is how people become homeless.

I'm terrified that I won't be able to scrape and claw my way out of this one.

Ziggy has had it up to here with living in the car in the city and is currently whining in the back.

I'm about to take him out using the leash I made from an old piece of rope I found on the sidewalk when a young man in a suit comes walking by.

I sit there and wait for him to pass, but he stops at my window, looking down at me behind those dark sunglasses.

"Are you living in this car?"

I don't look up at him. I don't answer. I'm too dead inside to answer.

"Do you want to make some quick money?" he asks.

Still no answer. It's best not to talk to anyone out here. They all just want to drag me down further.

"One million dollars for one day of work," he says as he reaches into his jacket and pulls out a black card. He hands it to me, but I still don't look at him. I just look ahead, hoping he'll leave. One million dollars? What a joke.

"I'll leave it here," he says as he tucks the business card in between my windshield and wiper. "In case you change your mind. Virgins only. Don't try to pull a fast one on us, we check."

"What?" I ask in disgust, but he's already walking away. Creep.

I look at the card through the windshield and my forehead scrunches up.

The Breeding Bidders Auction House.

What the hell is that?

CHAPTER THREE

Dylan

"AN AUCTION?" SCOTT SAYS AS HE CROSSES HIS ARMS OVER his chest and frowns. "For women?"

"I know it sounds barbaric," I say as I look at the dirt between us. "But the women agree to it."

"You're not going to find your mate there," he says in a harsh tone.

There's no way he's going to understand. Scott's grizzly was never a problem. Before he found his mate, he was as dangerous as Winnie the Pooh. Now that he has Rebecca, his grizzly is a total teddy bear.

He doesn't know what it's like to have an unstable wrecking ball ready to crash out of you and fuck up your life at any moment.

"It's not about finding my mate," I mutter with my eyes closed.

"There's Caleb," Scott says. "Let's see what he thinks of this."

"No, don't—"

"Caleb!" he shouts. "Get a load of this!"

Oh fuck.

My other brothers, Lionel and Nathan, come out of our huge family ranch house and come walking over too. Damn their enhanced shifter hearing.

"What is it?" Caleb asks when they all arrive. "Why are you wearing a suit? Is this about the bank manager calling?"

Goddammit. I just wanted to sneak out of here and go to the auction without having this conversation.

"Our brother here," Scott says in a derisive tone, "is going to an auction and guess what he's going to buy."

"A pair of balls?" Nathan says.

"A muzzle for his crazy bear?" Lionel guesses.

"Nope," Scott says as he looks at me. "You want to tell them?"

"I want to leave."

"He's going to an auction for women."

"I've heard about this," Caleb says. "Guys strip on stage and horny girls bid on them, but isn't that usually for charity?"

"*He's* doing the bidding," Scott says. "He's going to be bidding on girls."

"But what about your mate?" Nathan says, looking confused.

"What about her?" I snap. "She's not here. She might never be here. I'm not going to just let my bear descend into madness and take me along with him."

"But..." Caleb says, trying to understand. "With a girl who's not your mate? How can you even..."

"I don't expect you to understand," I snap as I yank open the door of my pickup truck. I don't even understand this myself. I don't want to do this. I'm sure I'm not even going to be able to go through with it when I get there, but I don't know what else to fucking do. My bear is going feral and I'm helpless to stop it.

Sometimes I think I should just let him go mad and gladly accept that bullet in my head. I might even do it myself before he gets too bad and I miss out on the opportunity.

They're all staring at me in disbelief as I start the engine and slam the door.

My blood is boiling as I peel out of our ranch, engulfing their shocked faces in a cloud of dust. I squeeze the steering wheel and grit my teeth, hating this, hating my bear, hating myself for being so fucking weak.

As I pull onto the highway, I know that I'm not going to go through with it. I'll never be with a girl who's not my fated mate. It's just not in me. It's not in any bear shifter. I can't. I won't. I don't want to.

But I'll go to the auction. Uncle Andrew pulled some strings to get me in and I don't want to let him down. Plus I don't want to go back to the ranch right now and see the concerned faces of my brothers as they try to awkwardly comfort me.

I reach down and shove the black leather bag full of cash under the passenger seat. I won't even bring it in.

I've never really needed too much money, so I have a lot of it. Our father left us his paid for ranch when he died and business has been good. With five shifters raising cattle and working the land, we get *a lot* done and make way more than we need. We're in the Montana wilderness and don't need much. We hunt, fish, and grow most of our food, we drive old pickup trucks, and none of us have an appetite for fancy things. Fancy things tend to get broken and when there's five grizzly bears around, *everything* gets broken eventually.

About three hours later, I arrive.

It's a huge white tent in the middle of a large stretch of plains with nothing around. No town, no farms, not even a fucking gas station.

On one side of the massive tent are a fleet of limousines and luxurious cars with the chauffeurs hanging around smoking cigarettes and chatting. On the other side of the tent is a makeshift runway with about a dozen private jets parked alongside it. I look up as another one comes dropping out of the evening sky and touches down on the hard packed dirt runway.

My old dirty pickup truck looks wildly out of place among these high-end cars. People turn to look at me when I get out, but they quickly look away when they see my size.

Bear shifters are all massive, especially grizzly bear shifters, and I'm the largest out of my brothers, so I'm used to people gawking and staring.

I hurry to the entrance of the tent and give the giant doormen my name. I sniff the air and smell lion. All three of them are lion shifters. My bear wakes up at the smell of cat and he begins to stir angrily.

"You in the wrong place, buddy?" the one with the crazy eyes asks. I'm guessing they don't get many shifters around here.

"My name is on the list, so I guess not." I walk in and he bumps me with his shoulder as I pass. My bear snarls low. I bite down the anger that's boiling up and head inside before we make an even bigger scene.

The seats are cloaked in darkness, hiding all of the rich perverts who've come to bid on virgins. With my shifter vision I can see all of them, but they can't see me. I'm happy for that as I slip into an empty seat near the back.

I inhale deeply, smelling the room. I can smell the money. The fancy soaps, the luxurious leather seats, the exhaust from private planes, the cigars, the cognac.

Another faint scent barely catches my attention, but when it does it refuses to let go. It tingles at first and then burns through my chest as it makes its way into my lungs.

My bear freezes. He's stunned as my heart starts beating harder.

It almost smells like… No. It can't be. My girl wouldn't be in a place like this. She'd be waiting for me.

As quickly as it came, the scent is gone. I can no longer smell it, but it's left me shaken. My hands are trembling as I grip the armrests, trying to keep it together.

It wasn't her. You're just nervous.

That must be it. My bear, however, doesn't seem so sure. He's pacing around, trying to get another whiff.

I turn my attention to the stage that's lit up with bright lights. There's a podium up there with *The Breeding Bidders Auction House* written on it and not much else.

I'm so far past having second thoughts about this experience. I'm on my twenty-third thoughts. I'd be leaving right now if that scent hadn't aroused my curiosity. I want to get another deep inhale of it.

My bear urges me to go investigate, but someone walks onto the stage and I stay in my seat. It's a well-dressed, rich-looking woman in her fifties with a blonde bob and features so severe they're as warm as an ice pick. Her icy blue eyes scan the crowd as she walks to the podium, but we're all in the darkness, so I'm wondering what she's actually seeing.

That must be my uncle's acquaintance, Coco St. James. I wonder how my uncle ever met her.

"Good evening," she says in a confident tone. "And welcome to The Breeding Bidders Auction House. All of the beautiful women you see tonight are here voluntarily. They're all verified virgins and are available to the highest bidder. If you place the winning bid, payment will be due immediately. Once payment has been received in full, you will be married on the spot to the lovely virgin of your choice."

A murmur of excitement ripples through the crowd as the green buttons on all the armrests light up. The bidding is about to start.

"The Breeding Bidders Auction House has been operating for thirty-five years, proudly serving the ultra-wealthy in sixty-two countries. We understand that your time is extremely valuable, so we will begin without further delay. Our first lovely young woman to be auctioned is Savannah Eastwood."

The door on the right of the stage opens and a pretty, but nervous-looking brunette walks in. She's wearing a sparkly baby blue gown with her curly hair flowing freely over her shoulders.

I look at this beautiful girl and think about what my uncle said. *Your bear is desperate to mate, but if he can't have his fated mate, he can keep his bear busy with someone else.*

I recoil in disgust from just thinking about touching her. How the hell could my uncle think this was anything but a horrible idea bound to fail?

I'm about to get up and storm out of here when that faint curious scent hits my nose again. My ass stays glued to the chair as my lungs smolder and burn from the beautiful scent.

This time, my bear doesn't freeze. He whimpers and whines to get out.

The bidding starts and so many green buttons get pushed that Coco has a hard time keeping up with them.

"Two point three million to the bidder in the back," Coco says with her voice racing. "Do we have two point five? Two point five to the bidder on the right. Two point seven to the bidder in the back. Do we have—Three million to the…"

The bidders drop off until it's just two eager bidders left in the fight. They keep upping each other's bids until the bid is over five million.

I glance back to get a look at one of them. He's about sixty or so, way too old for the beautiful girl in her early twenties on the stage, and about three hundred pounds. I wonder if that poor girl in blue realizes she's about to be wed to a man who probably can't walk up a flight of stairs without risking a heart attack.

The bidder in front finally wins out at a final bid of seven point one million dollars. He bounds up to the stage and steps out of the darkness. He's a young muscular man and appears to be Eastern European if I'd have to guess.

The girl's face lights up when she sees him and I can tell they're already falling in love. Coco explains that she's an ordained minister and marries them on the spot. The crowd politely claps as the two newlyweds leave through the door on the left.

The door on the right opens again and another girl comes out. I barely even look at her. I can't. My whole body is lighting up like I just chugged a gallon of gasoline and ate a match. My lungs are on fire. It's a sweet pain. A blissful burning. I can't get enough of it.

I can't even register what Coco is saying as a pounding thrashes in my ears. My bear is on full alert, but he's not angry like he normally is. He seems almost excited as he bounds around like a dog who was just told he's going on a walk.

This girl is bid off and then two more girls come out. Every time that door opens, I get another taste of that alluring scent.

Is she coming out here? Is she back there?

I can't stop my hands from shaking as I ask myself the question that matters the most.

Is she the one?

Is she my mate?

CHAPTER FOUR

Lucy

How the hell did I fall so far, so quickly? I'm still reeling in shock as I look around at all of the nervous girls with their thick makeup, fancy dresses, and high heels.

In minutes, I'll be ushered onto the stage and auctioned off like a piece of cattle.

I close my eyes and think back on the events leading up to this moment. I was living in my car and trying to wash up in the gas station bathroom when the attendant started banging on the door.

"Occupied," I yelled out, vowing to never take a shower for granted ever again.

"Someone is stealing your car," she said in a flat voice. I yanked open the door and can still remember the look of disgust in her eyes as she looked me up and down.

"Ziggy," I gasped as I ran past her into the parking lot.

My car was rolling down the street with my dog pacing in the back.

"Wait!" I screamed as I sprinted down the street after it. "My dog! Ziggy!!"

The brake lights lit up as the car stopped. I kept running even though it was so far away. The guy jumped out, opened the back door, and Ziggy ran out.

"Oh, thank God," I gasped as the thief jumped back into the car and peeled away with a cloud of black smoke puffing out of the exhaust. The little black card flew off the windshield and landed on the concrete as Ziggy sprinted in the other direction, ignoring my calls as he ran away from his now homeless, carless owner. I couldn't blame him for that. I was sinking fast and he didn't want to get pulled under with me.

With absolutely nothing to my name, I slowly walked over to the card, picked it up, and called the number.

"You're up next," one of the workers says as she comes over and fixes my hair. She has a headset on with a microphone. I look into her eyes as she fixes my dress and then touches up my makeup, but she doesn't look back at me. I'm not even a human to her. I'm a product. "Walk out the door and stand on the little X on the stage. Remember to smile. You have to smile or Coco will be *very* upset."

I don't even remember how to smile right now. I feel like I'm going to be sick all over my fancy new shoes.

They have me in a gorgeous white gown with a freaking diamond tiara in my hair. I look ridiculous. I've never in my life worn anything like this, but I guess I have to play the part.

She puts her palm on my lower back and practically pushes me toward the entrance of the stage. "You're on in thirty seconds," she says after someone squawks something in her earpiece. "Let me see your teeth."

I flash her my teeth and she seems satisfied.

"This is crazy, right?" I say to her.

She finally looks at me, seeing a person for the first time. "What do you mean?"

"An auction? Like, is this for real?"

The door opens and she pushes me onto the stage without answering.

I freeze for a second as the bright lights hit me and I see Coco's stern face staring at me. This is for real. This is *way* too real.

My head is spinning as I stumble toward the X on the stage. *Smile,* I tell myself. *Just keep smiling. It will be over in a minute.*

I'm forcing out a smile as my stomach twists into all kinds of knots. I thought being homeless was degrading, but washing off in a gas station bathroom has got nothing on this. *This* is humiliating.

I look out at the crowd, but all I see is a sea of darkness hiding all the dangerous creatures. What kind of men are in there? What kind of a man would be a part of something like this?

"This here is item number seven of the evening," Coco says like I'm some kind of antique at a flea market instead of a thinking, breathing person. "She has beautiful silky brown hair and radiant blue eyes. Notice the high cheekbones and the wide child-bearing hips."

I can feel my cheeks burning as I glance at the dark crowd, wondering what they're thinking. If they like what they see. If I'll get any bids.

"Remember," Coco says in a professional voice, "all of our girls are verified virgins."

I shudder as I remember the exam.

"We'll start the bidding at one million dollars," she says. "Do I have one million?"

A low deep growl rumbles through the place.

What the fuck was that?!

It sounded like a freaking werewolf or something.

There are murmurs as the men in the audience react to it. We are in the middle of nowhere. Maybe a bear wandered into the tent. I hope those security guards at the doors are carrying guns.

"One million," a deep voice grunts.

I shiver just from hearing it.

"One point one," another voice with a British accent says. He's on the other side of the room.

The growl returns, only it's louder and longer. The tiny hairs on my arms stand straight up as it vibrates through me.

"One point two million," the deep voice says. He's sounding more throaty and desperate like he's about to crack.

"One point three," the Brit counters.

"One point three million," Coco says, joining back in. "Do we have—"

"One point five," the low gravelly voice says.

"We have one point five to the gentleman on the—"

"One point eight," the Brit says.

The growl is back and it's so loud that the entire crowd stirs. I hear some footsteps quickly making their way to the exits.

"She's *mine*," the deep voice growls. "One point nine."

"We have one point nine million," Coco says, looking unfazed by the beast in the crowd. "Do we have two million?"

"I said she's *mine,*" the monstrous voice roars. "Bid again and I'll tear your fucking throat out. I'll marry her while you bleed out on the floor."

After that it's silence except for the pounding of my heart. What the hell is that thing? Am I his? Do I have to go home with it? Marry it?

I can't even breathe as I stare at the darkness, wondering what is out there waiting for me.

"Although we don't normally allow threats at The Breeding Bidders Auction House," Coco says calmly, "we'll stop the bidding here. Sold for one point nine million dollars to the gentleman with the deep voice. Please come up to the stage to wed your prize."

I can feel the tension in the room as heavy footsteps make their way up to the stage. My breath is lodged in my throat as I wait for my soon-to-be husband to present himself.

I gulp when I see the true size of his dark form approaching. He's massive. Monstrous. He can't be human. But if he's not, then what is he?

Even the always professional Coco sucks in a shocked breath beside me when my bidder steps into the light.

He's in a suit, but it's all torn up. Huge hulking muscles are bulging through the rips and tears in the fabric. He looks like a werewolf mid-phase with the short brown fur sprouting out of his skin and the long sharp canines pressing out against the inside of his lips. His fierce possessive eyes are locked on me. They're otherworldly. They're not human. They're glowing a shiny golden color with a practically feral gaze to them.

I should be running in terror. Fleeing in horror.

But I'm not. I'm standing here with my heart aching.

My whole body is being pulled to this half-man, half-beast. I can't take my eyes off him.

He's gorgeous. He's perfect. He's fucking mine.

I feel a wave of possession flow through me as I stare at him. I want him as badly as he wants me.

None of it makes any sense.

This guy is terrifying but I want to run to him and jump in his arms. I want to feel his big furry biceps wrapping around me, I want to feel the deep thud of his heart beating for me, I want to be close to those grotesque lips.

But... why?

CHAPTER FIVE

Dylan

I'M STILL IN SHOCK AS I STARE AT HER IN AWE. SHE'S EVEN more beautiful than I pictured. More delicate, more angelic, more awe-inspiring.

My feet move on their own as they carry me up the stairs of the stage. I'm so close. Her intoxicating scent is filling my lungs and mesmerizing my grizzly bear.

For the first time ever, he's motionless inside me. He's as stunned as I am.

I still can't believe she's here. My mate. I won't believe it until I touch her. A part of me thinks I might be dreaming. Maybe all those years without her has turned me crazy and I'm hallucinating all of this.

She doesn't flinch as I walk up to her, even though I'm mid-phase and looking like a monster. My suit is shredded to shit and my body is all swollen up. Even my fucking teeth are out. I didn't want her first impression of me to be like this, but what can I do? I'm not going to take my eyes off her now that I've finally found her.

She doesn't seem to mind my monstrous appearance at all. She's staring back at me in the same stunned way. Her sexy lips even curl up into a half smile as she looks up at me.

"What's your name?" I ask. My voice is always so deep and scratchy when I'm stuck mid-phase like this. It's not the impression I want to give, but I can't do a thing until my bear retreats back inside me and he's too busy inhaling her scent to move.

"Lucy," she says in a low voice. "And you?"

"*Dylan*," I growl. "We're mates, sweet girl. You're all mine. Always have been."

She swallows hard as she watches me with those curious brown eyes. I can see it clicking in her mind. All of those years with no physical attraction to anyone. No desire to kiss a boy or to hold hands or do any of the other things boys surely tried to get her to do.

It was all because she belonged to me. Because her soul was waiting for me. Her body was craving me. Her mind is the last to realize it, but it's realizing it now. She's always been mine and now she knows it.

"The payment..." Coco says as the three lion shifter guards approach the stage.

I have to hold back my protective bear as we notice them hovering around. He's extra feisty now that his mate is in front of us.

"The payment is..." God, she's beautiful. I can't even get through a fucking sentence without being distracted by her beauty. She's stunning. All the waiting, all of the frustration, all of the agony, for all those years... it was all worth it. Worth it for this angel to arrive. Worth it to be standing in front of her, admiring her perfection. I'd go through it again and again if I knew she was waiting for me at the end of it.

"Sir," Coco says, jerking me out of my daze. "The payment."

"In my truck," I mutter out. "The white one covered in mud. You can't miss it."

"Sergio," Coco says to one of the guards. He steps forward with his hand out.

"What?" I growl.

"The keys, sir," he says. "I'll fetch the payment for you."

I shove my hand into my pocket, yank out my keys, and dump them into his palm. As he leaves with them, I start to panic.

I don't have enough.

I only have about two hundred thousand in the truck and owe one point nine million.

They can't stop me from taking her. I'll tear every throat out in this place if it's the only way I can get my girl to safety. Nothing or no one is going to stop me.

"Please stand here," Coco says, shifting us to the spot on the stage where she performs the wedding ceremony.

"Now, take her hand," Coco says when we're standing in front of each other at the spot.

We reach out and gently take each other's hands. My heart nearly stops. She's touching thick fur on my swollen fingers, but she doesn't even flinch. She doesn't seem to mind at all.

I'm already obsessed with this girl. I can feel the obsession growing through me like strong roots of an old oak tree, slithering and spreading itself inside my body where it will be unmovable. Unshakable. Permanent.

"Marry us," I growl. "*Hurry*."

My bear is getting impatient. Hell, *I'm* getting impatient. I want her now. In every way. I want to throw her over my shoulder, take her out of here, and get started on our honeymoon. I want to tear that dress off her sweet supple body and claim her tight warm cunt. I've been waiting long enough for it and I'm done waiting.

"There are no marriages until payment is received in full," Coco says.

A whiff of lion hits my nose as the guard returns with my bag of cash. "Bad news," he says. "Only two hundred and ten thousand in here."

Coco frowns as she peeks into the bag at the stacks of crisp hundred dollar bills. I would have found two million if I knew. Hell, I would have robbed a dozen banks to get the cash. I would have done anything I had to.

"That's all I got," I tell her. My bear starts stirring inside me, snarling angrily at the interruption. If she doesn't let this girl go at a discount, then I'm going to let him out. He'll tear the place apart while getting Lucy to safety. "I strongly suggest you take it."

"I got the one point nine million," the British guy says with his hand in the air. He's in the darkness, but I can see him. I can tear him to shreds and the three bodyguards he's flanked by. "I'll buy her."

Fuck it. Let's do this the hard way.

I start to let my bear come through. My body grows as a deep snarl rumbles out of my mouth.

"Two hundred and ten should be fine," Coco says nervously when she sees that a furious grizzly bear is about to explode out of me in the middle of her auction. "It appears they're already in love and who am I to keep lovers apart?"

She must know about shifters since she hired three of them as guards. She must know that Lucy and I are fated mates and that keeping us apart will get ugly fast. Plus, I'm sure she doesn't want to end the night so early. Not when she has a room full of billionaires and a back room full of young virgins to auction off.

The three lion shifters are watching me closely, but I'm only watching her. Lucy is a goddess and I keep forgetting to breathe in her presence. I'm studying every inch of her —the slope of her eyebrows, the curve of her adorable nose, her soft round cheeks—while Coco quickly marries us.

"I now pronounce you husband and wife," she says as my heart soars. Getting married isn't even necessary since we're mates and connections don't get any deeper than that, but I'll still take it. I want to be attached to this incredible woman in every possible way.

"You may now kiss the bride."

I can feel her hands shaking in mine as we both lean in. Our lips connect and I nearly die on the spot. Her mouth is so soft, her breath so sweet. It's a soft, gentle, closed-mouth kiss that I want to savor forever. But there's a room full of perverts watching and I'm not about to give them the satisfaction. I'll whisk her out of here and do all of the dirty things swirling through my mind in private. Our union is for us alone.

We rush down the steps of the stage hand in hand as husband and wife. The lion shifter hands me my keys with a dirty look. I stare him down as I grab them, then grab my wife, and then leave. I'm gripping her wrist tight as I pull her through the darkness toward the door in the front.

I don't slow down until we're at my truck. Then, I turn

and slowly look her up and down once more. I can't believe she's mine.

"Thank you, Dylan," she says in a soft sweet voice that nearly has my knees buckling.

"For what?"

"For saving me," she says as she licks those plump pink lips. "For getting me out of there."

My bear has retreated inside, letting me take over. I guess even he's smart enough to know that he's cramping my style with all of the ripped clothes and long fur.

"You're with me from now on," I tell her as I put a protective arm around her shoulder. "Always."

"Hey!" a deep aggressive voice calls out through the parking lot.

I turn and growl when I see the British man storming over with his three guards by his side. They're human, not even shifters, so this should be fucking fun.

"Get out of here," I warn as my bear perks up. "You won't get a second chance to walk away. She's mine and I'm not giving her up."

It's pissing me off that these fools even think they can take her away. I should kill their boss simply for having the gall to try and take what's mine.

"Do you know who I am?" the Brit asks with a sneer. "I get *whatever* I want and I want *her*."

I pull her protectively behind my back. "Close your eyes, Lucy. I don't want you to see this."

"It's okay, Dylan. I can handle it."

I'm about to argue with her, but my bear comes bursting out.

Shit, I mutter as I get pulled in. He explodes out of me in a vicious snarl and all I can do is watch from deep inside as he charges at them.

One of the guards runs. Smart.

The other two, however, draw their guns. My bear gets shot in the front leg three times, but he's in such a frenzied state that he doesn't seem to notice. He doesn't slow down at all.

I watch as he lunges on one, slamming him into the pavement with his big paws on the man's chest. It breaks every bone in his torso, leaving him dead on the spot.

The third bodyguard sees this and fires his gun wildly as he sprints away.

Only the Brit left. He's glaring at me as he draws his gun.

This one is mine, I tell him. *Let me out.*

My bear is reluctant, but he lets me pull him back in.

I burst out of him, flexed and naked. Blood is leaking out of the three bullet holes on my left arm. The pain is searing hot, but it doesn't stop me.

"I warned you, I'd tear your throat out," I tell him in a low controlled voice. "You should have stayed inside."

He points his gun at my forehead. "And you should have known your place. What kind of man doesn't have two million dollars?"

"I don't need money," I snarl. "I have my mate."

"Not for long, you don't. Lucy come—"

Just the sound of my girl's name on his filthy lips snaps something loose inside me. Something protective and unstoppable. I dip down and lunge forward.

He recoils with a gasp. The gun goes off but the bullet flies harmlessly over my head.

Long black claws tear out of my fingertips as I swipe my curled hand through the air at the arrogant billionaire. My claws slice through his throat, spraying hot blood everywhere.

His eyes widen and go cold as he clutches his throat like he's trying to keep the blood from spilling out. He coughs up a mouthful of blood and then drops to the ground, dead.

With my shoulders heaving and my eyes shining a bright gold, I turn to my mate. I'm expecting her to take one look at the monster I have hiding inside and scream. I'm expecting her to run away, wanting nothing to do with me, but she just stands there, staring.

It's not repulsion and fear I see in her eyes. It's love. Devotion. Gratitude.

I think she's the first person to ever understand me. To truly understand me.

"Your… Your arm…" she says, stammering over her words. I notice that her hands are shaking as she looks at my bloody bicep. "I have to get you to a hospital."

I know it looks bad. Three bullet holes in my bicep are spewing out blood, but I can take the pain. I can take anything with her by my side.

"Where are the keys?" she says as she opens the driver's door of my truck. "Get in. Hurry. I'll drive you to a hospital."

I twist my arm and pinch the skin around one of the bullet holes, grunting and wincing as I grab the metal slug. I pinch and roll it, working it up until it slides back out of the hole and drops to the dirt.

"Did you just…?" she asks, shocked at the horrifying sight of me performing self-surgery.

I turn around so she can't see me take out the other two. I've given her enough disturbing images already, I don't need to give her two more.

Once the bullets are out, I head over to the truck. I grab

my shredded pants off the ground and take out my keys and wallet.

"You can't drive like that!" she says in a near frantic voice.

"Naked?" I ask with a grin.

"Bleeding! You have three bullet holes in your arm!"

"You're more of a distraction to me than the pain."

She looks around in a panic. "We have to get you to a hospital!"

"It's okay," I say softly as I walk over to the passenger's side and open the door for her. "I'll be fine."

She doesn't move. "How?"

"They're already starting to heal," I tell her. "By the time I get you back to my place, they will be nothing but faded pink holes."

She hesitates but then walks over and gets into the truck. I sniff the air one last time, getting one deep smell of her before I close the door.

I open the door to the back and grab my extra pair of jeans on the backseat. Bear shifters always have to keep extra clothes around, but for anyone with a bear like mine, it's a necessity.

Which makes me realize…

He's quiet. He's calm. He's not thrashing around or stewing with anger. He's like an old dog sleeping in front of a roaring fire in the middle of a cold winter afternoon.

I can't believe it.

With my heart pounding and my future looking bright, I get into the truck to get my mate out of this horrible place.

CHAPTER SIX

Lucy

My eyes are locked on the dark highway as it rolls under us, but all I want to do is turn to the side and stare at Dylan. Everything about him is intriguing.

The man literally turned into a grizzly bear to save me from those men back there. He got shot three times and then plucked out the bullets with his fingers. He's the size of an ogre and as hot as an A-list actor.

But more intriguing then all of that is the yearning fire he stokes in my core. I want him so badly. I want him to claim me, to have all of me, to be *deep* inside me. I don't understand any of it. I've never had feelings like this before. Not even close.

A spot on my neck starts tingling as we pass a few cars. I touch the spot under my left ear, but the tingling only grows stronger. It feels… weird. Like it's missing something. Like *I'm* missing something. I can't explain it, I've never felt anything like this before.

Dylan lets out a low rumbling sound as he watches me. "That's where my mark belongs."

"Am I your... mate?" I ask with a hard swallow. "You're a bear shifter, right?"

"I am," he says in that deep sexy voice I find irresistible. "And yes, Lucy. We're mates."

Mates... I don't even know what to think about that. I'm still trying to wrap my head around the fact that this mysterious stranger is my husband. So much has changed in the past hour. My entire life has been flipped upside down.

"What does that mean?" I ask with a tremble. "What do I have to do?"

He looks at me and the ferocious intensity in his warm green eyes makes me shiver all over. I barely know him, but I do know that he would do anything for me. He would kill to protect me. He already has.

"You just have to be yourself," he says as his eyes roam down my body before turning back to the road. My pussy pulses with heat in response. "Follow your heart. Don't fight it."

"Fight what?"

"That feeling that's coursing through your body. Do you feel it? The yearning for me. The pull toward me. The craving. The need?"

He looks at me and all I can do is nod. How does he know? It's like he's spying inside my head.

"If you think it's strong for you," he says with a deep inhale, "you should feel what it's like for me."

"I'm sorry," I say. I don't want anyone to feel like they're forced to be with me.

"No," he says in a fierce tone. "That's not what I meant at all. I'm so happy I finally found you, Lucy. I've been searching for you for decades. Nothing has made me happier than having you by my side."

We sit in silence as I fidget with my hands in my lap. This is a lot to process. I'm trying to think it through but it's hard with all of these naughty things whipping through my mind.

Dirty thoughts keep distracting me… Thoughts like Dylan pulling over and climbing on top of me… Hiking my dress up and tearing my panties off with those strong hands… Grunting in my ear as he thrusts his big hard cock deep into my virgin pussy… Sinking his teeth into my neck and marking me as his own…

"So, the mark," I say, touching my neck again. "You have to bite me?"

He shifts in his seat as his face gets all tight and uncomfortable. "Well… It's best not to think about that right now. I won't mark you tonight."

I should feel relief over this, but I'm kind of feeling disappointment instead. It feels like his mark belongs on me and I won't be complete until it's there.

"Okay," I whisper as I let my eyes roam over his huge shirtless body. I'm a bit braver now, letting my eyes linger on all of the good parts.

His arms are *jacked*. All hard curves of his beautiful biceps and strong triceps. His chest is moving up and down with every breath, flexing his stomach with every exhale.

I swallow hard as I slide my eyes up his thick muscular neck and onto his face. He really is gorgeous. I could stare at that face for *hours* and I think I'm going to be lucky enough to be able to. He has a big masculine jaw with soft tender lips. Eyes as mesmerizing as a crystal ball and messy brown hair that I want to sink my hands in.

All of that is sexy beyond belief, but what's really got me intrigued is what he's packing below his waist. I saw *all* of him when he changed back into his human form after attacking the bodyguards with his grizzly bear.

Between his big muscular thighs was a long thick cock that made my mouth water. Even under the deadly threat of a gun pointed at me, I still craved it with a carnal desire. I *needed* it.

I shift in my seat as my pussy begins to throb. I'm already so wet. I can feel my need soaking through my panties.

Dylan inhales deeply and I watch as the tiny hairs on his arms rise.

I remember reading somewhere that bear shifters have enhanced senses. Can he… *smell* me down there? Does he know how aroused I am?

The truck drifts over the line and hits those bumpers in the concrete that are designed to jerk sleepy drivers awake. It works on us. We both jump to attention.

Dylan steers back into the middle of the lane and grips the steering wheel with white knuckles. There's no one else around on this long country road. It's like we're the only two people left in the universe. That's how it feels anyway.

"Are you okay?" I ask when I see his arms flex.

He runs his hand over his face and then nods, but I can tell he's struggling with something.

"I'm okay." He's lying. I can already tell. I already feel like I know him so well. "It's just… It's hard."

"What's hard?"

"To concentrate with you beside me. Looking at the

road when all I want to do is memorize every stunning detail of you. To have our bodies so close, yet feel so far away."

I say it before I chicken out.

"We don't have to be so far away," I say with a throaty voice. "We're mates... And husband and wife... We can be... close."

He looks at me with a smoldering fire in those sexy green eyes and then jerks the truck onto the side of the road.

I gulp as he turns the engine off, leaving the warm blue lights on the dashboard. It lights up his face in a blue glow, giving him an ethereal look. *Wow*. I can't believe this man is *my* mate.

He's so enormous that he practically takes up the entire cabin of the truck. It might just be my imagination, but it feels like the truck dips as he leans over onto my side.

My chest flutters as our eyes connect with some hot, deep, and prolonged eye contact. I look at his lips and my mouth waters.

The air around us suddenly feels like it's charged with something electric. I can feel the crackling in the air.

"Close is good," he whispers. He's so close now that I can feel his hot minty breath tickling my lips. I lean in as my chin tilts up.

I'm giving off some strong 'kiss me' vibes and Dylan picks up on them and delivers in a big way. He cups my jaw with a strong hand and pulls me toward his mouth as he leans down and kisses me hard.

I moan as our lips connect and he thrusts his hot tongue into my mouth. This isn't a soft romantic kiss like we had back at the auction house. This one is all possession. It's intense and needy like he's claiming my mouth as his own.

It's his. It's all fucking his.

If he can kiss me like this every day, then he can have it.

His strong hands move down my neck and over my shoulders, gripping me in a territorial way that tells me he's never going to want to let me go.

"Oh, Dylan," I moan as his incredible lips kiss a soft trail down my neck. I'm *burning* for him. I need to feel him everywhere.

He groans as I grab his big hands and shove them onto my breasts. "*Yes,*" I moan as he squeezes and massages them over my dress, making me throb even deeper. "Touch them. Touch me anywhere you want."

I grab his muscular arms as his strong hand slides up my inner thigh, dipping under my dress. My legs part, opening wide for him.

"I know you kept this little pussy safe for me," he growls as he kisses along my collarbone. "I don't even have to ask if you're a virgin or not. I know you're untouched."

"How do you know?" I gasp as that magical hand gets closer and closer to the throbbing. It's unbearable now. I *need* to be touched and the fucker is taking his time, teasing me, prolonging the agony. He must feel the heat. He must know how desperate I am for him.

"That's how it is for mates," he says as he kisses the top of my chest. I drop my head back on the leather seat as I spread my legs further apart. "I know you waited because I waited. Tonight was the first time I ever kissed a girl."

"Well, you're already a pro," I say as I melt into the

seat, desperate to feel him on my sex. I'm aching all over. It's fucking agony…

"I'm going to treat this hot little pussy so good," he growls as his hand finally arrives. I moan hard as he slides his fingers over my mound and presses his fingertip over my opening. My wet panties are stopping him from dipping in, but it still sends bursts of heat pulsing through my body.

"This pussy belongs to me," he says in a deep authoritative voice as he peels my panties to the side. My heart is beating so fast. He's so damn close.

My eyes fall closed as his hand connects, skin on skin this time. He rubs my pussy and dips his finger in, groaning like a beast as he does it. I turn into a puddle on the seat as he plays with my sex, rubbing my aching clit with quick firm circles and sliding his fingers through my folds.

"Fuck," I gasp as he sticks two thick fingers in, sliding them up to his knuckles. I already feel so full, so complete like this. How am I going to fit his huge cock inside me?

He slides them out and I feel an immediate sense of loss. I'm wanting him back in me as I watch him lift his dripping wet fingers and suck them clean. He doesn't stop until he's sure he's got every drop and only then does he slide his hand back under my dress to rock my world some more.

My legs start trembling as he fingers me harder, faster. Heat and tightness coil within me. I feel like I'm going to burst.

"Cum on my hand, sweet girl," he orders in a firm voice. "I want to feel your pussy gushing all over me."

He thrusts his two fingers back into my wet hole and

presses against my aching clit, massaging it with the base of his palm while I scream and convulse on the seat.

The tightness snaps and I cum hard. All over him.

I'm thrashing around and crying out as wave after wave of blissful heat surges through me. When the last of the orgasm flows out of me and onto his fingers, he pulls his soaked hand away and licks it clean once again.

I'm breathing heavily as I watch him. He's so fucking sexy. Those wet lips and sexy tongue are licking my juices off his fingers with an eagerness that grips my attention and squeezes my core.

The need is still there but some of the desperation is gone as I sit back in my seat.

"I'm not going to take your cherry here," he says in a breathless tone. "I want to more than anything, but it won't be like this. Not in my truck. Not on the side of the road. My mate deserves the best and although I might not be able to give you the absolute best, I'm going to damn near try."

"I just want you," I whisper. "It doesn't matter where."

"It matters to me," he says with a half smile. "I'm not going to claim you where I stick my grocery bags."

I chuckle as I gaze at him through half-closed, glazed-over eyes. For some reason I have a hard time picturing this guy grocery shopping. For sure he's able to carry all of his bags in one trip.

I start to wonder about him... How much he eats... His weekly grocery bill must be in the thousands of dollars.

"You're staying with me now," he says as he sits back in his seat. "I have a ranch in Montana. Horses, mountains, a river, you'll love it."

"It sounds incredible," I say, unable to even picture it. I've always wanted to see Montana. I love the mountains.

"Where do you live? I can drive you there so you can grab some things."

My cheeks tingle as my face heats up with shame. I don't want to tell him that I'm homeless. I don't want him to know what a loser I am.

He has this image of me as a princess with this gorgeous white dress on and I don't want to break it with the cruel reality of my situation. I want him to always look at me the way he's looking at me now.

"Lucy?" he asks when I don't answer. "Where do you live?"

My chin trembles as I look down at my fidgeting hands. "I... don't have a place."

"You're crashing with a friend?"

"No. I'm... homeless."

"Homeless?" he repeats like that was the last word he was expecting to hear.

I shrug as I give him a sad smile.

"I had a rough year."

"You... You're living on the street?"

"Still think I'm the girl for you?" I ask with a bitter edge. It's not fair, I know. I guess I'm trying to ice him out before he rejects me.

"Absolutely," he says with a fierce resolve that makes my heart ache. "There's no doubt. And you're not homeless anymore, sweet girl. You'll always have a place by my side. That I promise and you can count on me."

I know I can. He's already given me so much.

Safety. Security. Stability.

He's given me exactly what I need.

And when we get back to his place, I'm going to give him exactly what he needs.

CHAPTER SEVEN

Lucy

My body is still vibrating like a tuning fork as Dylan pulls his truck onto his ranch. He drives up to a huge beautiful house nestled in the darkness that's lit up with soft lights. I'm burning with desire as he parks beside the house next to a few other cars and trucks.

I want to ask who these other vehicles belong to, but I can't seem to speak or focus on anything but him. On what's about to happen and how much I want it.

His big hand turns the key, shutting the engine off, and my breath quickens. I can still feel his hand down there and the promise of feeling more is getting me all fluttery.

"I can't wait to be inside you," he says as he looks at me with dark possessive eyes. "I've been waiting for this moment for *years*. There are so many things I want to do to you and I'm going to do them all."

"Like what?" I ask with a shaky voice. I don't know what he has in mind, but I'm game for all of it.

"Like spreading your legs wide open and burying my hungry mouth in your dripping wet pussy," he says in a low calm voice. "I'm going to make a mess of your pretty little cunt. I'm going to fill it with cream. You'll be *dripping* with me once I'm done with you."

I swallow hard as I watch the intensity in his eyes. My eyes drop down to his lap and I nearly gasp when I see the size of his erection straining behind his pants. He's so *thick*. And long. Holy fuck.

"You want it, don't you?"

I nod my head, unable to speak.

"Come then," he says as he runs a hand through his hair. "Come upstairs and I'll show you how fucking hard you make me."

We both hurry out of the truck and meet at the front bumper.

"No running away now," he says with a sly grin before he grabs my waist and tosses me over his shoulder like I weigh nothing at all.

My pussy is aching as he carries me into the house and up the stairs. There's only a light on in the kitchen and if anyone else lives here, they seem to be all asleep. It is after one in the morning and this is a ranch, so they're probably all early risers.

He carries me down the hall and into his room. It's a nice cozy space with a big bed, a fireplace, and a bathroom beside the large dresser. There's a few large windows along one wall that probably have a spectacular view, but right now all I can see out of them is darkness.

My man lowers me onto the bed and kisses me hard on

the lips before leaving to close the door. The heat throbs between my legs as he locks the door with a click.

He stops short when he turns around and sees me laying on the bed. "Fuck," he groans in a low voice. "You're spectacular. Perfect in every possible way."

I suck in a breath as I fluff up my hair. I'm wondering how I look right now all splayed out on the bed with this gorgeous dress fanned out at my feet. He's looking at me like I'm the most beautiful thing he's ever seen.

He's the most beautiful thing I've ever seen standing there in nothing but his blue jeans. He's not wearing a belt or underwear so the jeans are low on his hips, showing off the top of his pubic hair and the beautifully carved V on his pelvis. My mouth waters as my eyes work their way up, admiring his deep six-pack and sexy navel. His chest is so massive. It looks incredibly powerful as he watches me with a look of awe.

I never thought I could get a man like this. One who is so physically imposing. His arms are bigger than my thighs. He looks like he could pick this bed off the ground with me in it and spin it over his head like a basketball.

I gulp as he comes back into the moment and reaches for the button on his jeans. "You ready to see how crazy you make me?"

"*Yes*," I say, barely able to get it out in a whisper. "I want to see it."

He grins as he pops the button out, then hesitates. "You first," he says. "You already saw mine. Fair's fair."

"You want to see…" I can't even say the dirty words in front of him. I'm too shy. My cheeks are burning.

"Your pussy," he says, not shy at all. "Pull that dress up and let me see your soaked panties."

I'm shy, but I'm aroused too and the desire wins out. I

slowly pull my dress up my legs until it's bunched at the waist and he can see my wet underwear.

He licks his lips as his eyes focus between my legs. "Underwear off," he demands.

"Don't you want to do that part?"

"No." He shakes his head. "I want you to do it. I want you to show me."

I take a deep breath and then hook my fingers into the elastic waistband. This is my mate. My husband. I can show him every part of me without judgment or shame. I *want* to show him every part of me.

With a burst of courage, I pull my underwear down my shaky thighs and slide them off my feet.

Dylan lets out a low growl as I spread my legs apart once again, only this time, I'm not hiding anything.

"Fucking hell," he groans as he stares in stunned fascination. "What a beautiful pussy. No wonder I've been desperate to find you."

The way he's standing there staring, I think he's going to make me wait forever.

"Your turn."

He gives me a sexy grin as he drops his zipper and then drops his jeans. *Oh my god...* His *huge* hard cock springs up and slaps his pelvis, splattering pre-cum beside his navel.

A deep sensual craving takes over my body as I watch him wrap his strong hand around his shaft. He steps out of his jeans and approaches the bed.

I jump up to my hands and knees, my dress falling back down around me. I don't care what he has planned, we're not doing anything until I get that delicious-looking cock in my mouth.

He's about to protest, but I smack his hand away, grab

his thick dick, and pucker my lips. When he sees my fingers wrapped around his hard shaft, he forgets what he was going to say and lets me take over instead.

It feels even bigger in my hand. The thing is enormous.

I squeeze his shaft and a bead of pre-cum oozes out of the tip.

"Lick that up, baby," he groans as he watches me.

I lick it up and moan at his sweet succulent taste.

"You like that?"

I nod as I stare at his cock.

"Then put it in your mouth, sweet girl. I got more of it waiting for you."

My pussy is pulsing with heat as I slide his big swollen head between my lips. I have to stretch my jaw wider and wider as I push him further into my mouth.

More pre-cum slides onto my tongue and I get another delicious taste. *"Mmmmm,"* I moan until he's in so deep that I start choking.

He grins at me as I pull it back an inch or two.

"Get used to being stuffed, baby," he says with a satisfied smirk. "I'm going to be filling every sexy hole you have."

"I can't wait for that," I say with a seductive smile.

He drops his head back and groans as I swirl my tongue around his shaft and then glide it up to his head. My hand is clenched around the thick base of his dick as I slide my flat tongue up the back of his shaft. He shivers. I grin, loving that I can make this big growly alpha of a shifter tremble like that.

His hands slide into my hair as I start sucking him off again. I relax my jaw and let him move my mouth up and down his length at the speed he likes.

This is so fucking hot. I'm *drenched*. I can feel the sticky heat slipping onto my thighs as I coat this big dick with my tongue.

I look up at him with lustful eyes, letting him know that I'm loving every second of this. He looks back down at me with intense green eyes, looking at me like he can't get enough of the erotic view.

"You want me to cum in your slutty little mouth?" he asks in a deep throaty voice.

"*Yes*," I gasp between sucks. "I want to *taste* it."

His grip on my head tightens as he carefully pumps his hips forward, sliding his dick into the back of my throat.

"I was planning on saving it for your ripe little cunt, but I have a lifetime of hot cum built up for you. Keep your jaw slack."

I do as he says, trying to keep my jaw relaxed as he starts fucking my mouth harder. Faster. I grab onto his ass, trying to hold him inside of me with every thrust, but he's too powerful and he pulls back before ramming it back in me.

My throat burns, my eyes water, but it feels *so* good. I'm finally feeling stuffed and full like I've always craved.

"I'm going to cum," he growls as he grabs a fistful of my hair. I moan as he tilts my head so he can slide in deeper. I feel him deep in the back of my throat when he cums hard, releasing his hot cum all over my slutty little mouth.

I start gasping and choking, so he pulls out of me. *Noooo*. I want him back in. I don't want him to go.

I moan as I swallow him down, loving this new feeling of being so full of my man. The heat travels down into my chest as I lick my lips and try to reach for him again.

He steps out of my reach with a shake of his head.

"You've had your taste, baby. Now it's my turn to taste

that sweet dripping cunt. Lie back on the bed, spread your legs, and pull that dress up. I'm going to tongue that pussy until you cum all over my mouth."

He comes forward as I do what he says. I drop onto the bed, lift up my dress, spread my legs, and prepare to have the experience of a lifetime…

CHAPTER EIGHT

Dylan

I've been smelling her wet pussy all night, but up close, nose right next to her glistening pink folds… *fuuuuccccckkk.* It's the most enticing scent I've ever had the pleasure of coming across. It ignites my body. It sets my insides on fire.

She moves on the bed with a little moan, wiggling her hips as she brings her sex closer to my mouth. I fucking adore the sexy noises she makes. I can hear the desire in them and it's making my heart race.

It's the prettiest pussy I've ever seen. Ripe and fresh with sweet juice slowly leaking out of her virgin-tight hole.

I'm trying to hold myself back, to admire it for a few more seconds. It's the last time it's going to be like this—virgin-tight, untouched, pure—and I want to get a good long look at it before I sully it forever with my big throbbing cock.

My bear is rumbling inside of me, urging me to take it. To claim what is ours by fate and by birthright.

She rolls her hips as she massages her tits with a moan. What little resolve and restraint I had leaves me and I lunge on her delicious cunt with one long, slow, lap of my tongue.

Her body shudders as she feels my mouth on her. Her legs start shaking around me, but all I can focus on is the sweet juicy cunt on my tongue. I slide it up her soft folds until I get to her hard clit. She cries out as I flick it with my tongue and trace circles around the base.

"Oh, Dylan," she moans as she squeezes her tits hard. "Oh, fuck, it feels so good."

I slide my tongue back down and plunge it into her tight hole. Once I taste her insides, I turn into an animal, devouring her cunt with a wild frenzy.

I'm moaning like a beast as I swallow down every drop of pussy juice she gives me. My hands are on the back of her thighs, lifting them and spreading them as wide as they'll go. I'm probably being too rough, but I can't seem to stop myself. I want to see all of her. I want every inch of her exposed to me.

I lean back, mouth and chin dripping with her, and take a second to stare at her cunt. Her pussy lips are all puffy red, her beautiful asshole looking so damn tight. She gasps as I lean down and give it all a deep lick.

Her hands are massaging her tits over her white dress as I devour her. I've been wanting to see those sweet things all night and I'm done waiting.

"Pull that dress down for me, baby," I growl between licks. "Pop those big tits out for your man."

She wiggles her shoulders as she pulls the straps down. My tongue is buried in her hole, but my eyes are on her chest as she yanks her dress down and those juicy tits come into view.

"Fuck," I growl on her cunt as I reach up and grab one. It's so soft with her hard pink nipple digging into my palm. I feel the other one, but then grab her legs once they start to slowly close. I yank them back open and keep them spread apart as I continue to tongue her needy little pussy.

She starts writhing on the bed, moving to the rhythm of my tongue. Once I slide my lips back up to her clit and start sucking on it, I can tell she's close to cumming.

I grab a big breast in each hand, sucking her pussy as her legs squeeze closed against the sides of my head.

The rhythm and intensity get her and she cums hard all over me. I grin as I hear her scream, but that grin disappears as warm pussy juice washes over my lips. I lick it all up as my hard cock aches and drips pre-cum on the floor.

She's trembling and whimpering my name after the peak of her orgasm. I grab my dick and stand up, watching her succumbing to the intense pleasure. Her eyes are closed, tits swaying with every heavy breath, hands clenched around the bedsheets.

All of her best parts are out, but I want her completely naked when I claim her. She barely notices as I grab her dress and pull it off.

She's spectacular. It still stuns me that I've been able to live without her for this long. How did I even function without this incredible girl?

No wonder my bear went crazy. I'm surprised I held on for this long and kept my sanity.

Well, the wait is over. She's here now and she's not going anywhere.

I squeeze my hard shaft as I climb onto the bed. Her legs are spread wide open, looking like they don't have an ounce of energy left in them after that crushing orgasm.

She turns her head and looks at me with glazed-over eyes as I drag the thick head of my cock up her wet slit.

"Oh, Dylan," she moans. "Put it in me."

There's no talk of contraception, no talk of protection. She doesn't need protection from me. I'm going to cum *deep* in her pussy, as close to her ripe womb as I can, and once I'm done, she'll have my baby growing inside her.

I'm going to *breed* this girl over and over again. The thought of getting her pregnant makes my balls ache with desire. I can't wait to see her stomach round with my child.

The intense urge to breed her takes over and I guide the head of my dick to her virgin hole. She clenches her teeth and sucks in a breath as I add some pressure.

"I got you, baby," I whisper to her as I slowly push my head in. Her warm wet pussy engulfs me as I push my hips a little more.

I close my eyes, marveling at the tightness, whimpering at the heat. She feels so fucking good. This is where I belong. In this cunt. With this girl.

"Hold on, baby," I warn her. "I'm going to thrust in hard."

Her fingertips curl into my arms as I hold myself over her. I take one last look at her pure angelic face and then thrust my hips hard, plunging my cock *deep* inside her.

She screams out as her nails dig into my flesh.

Oh, fuck. Her pussy is so damn tight. It's squeezing me

with the most blissful kind of pain. I take a few deep breaths, holding myself inside her as I get used to the tightness.

She's getting used to my tremendous size; only she's having a harder go of it. Her back is arched, her jaw clenched shut, fingers squeezed tight around the bedsheets.

I lean down and start kissing her breasts to distract her. She moans as I slide my tongue up to her nipple and take it into my mouth. Her pussy starts to relax around my cock as I suck on one nipple then the other.

"You feel so good," I growl as I lean back up on my arms. The view from above her is incredible—golden hair splayed out on the bed, big tits heaving up and down, her beautiful brown eyes looking up at me with trust and love. I drag my eyes down to where we're connected and moan at the sight of her soft golden hair.

I watch as I slowly drag my cock out of her cunt. Pink cream covers my shaft and the sight of her virginity on me makes me feel like the luckiest man on earth.

She's still digging her nails into my arms as I pull back until just the tip of my cock is still in her. With a hard grunt, I thrust it back in.

"You're doing great," I whisper to her as I start thrusting in and out at a slow steady pace. "How is your pussy feeling?"

"So good," she moans as her fingernails ease out of my skin. Her hands slide down to my ass and she starts pulling me into her with every thrust. "Your dick is *amazing*."

I start fucking her harder and faster, loving the way her tits are bouncing around with every slam of my dick.

"*Yes!*" she cries out. "Fuck, yes! Like that. *Harder!*"

I've been holding back. Taking it easier on her. But as she begs me for more, I realize that I don't have to. She's my mate and she can take whatever I give her. This pussy was made for my cock and it can handle every thrust of my big dick.

"That's my girl," I growl as I grab her leg and hoist it over my shoulder. I plunge my dick back into her pussy and it hits even deeper. She cries out, but I don't stop.

All I can think about is breeding this warm juicy cunt. I fuck her harder and faster until we're both on the edge of cumming.

"Cum on my dick," I growl in a voice that's only half-human. "Cum all over me."

She cries out as her orgasm hits, clinging to me as the heat overtakes her. I watch her shaking and trembling under me as her eyes cloud over, but it's only when I feel her pussy pulsating on my shaft and milking my cock that I cum too.

It rips through me in a blaze of heat, scorching through my veins as I thrust in as far as my cock will go. She moans hard as I release every drop of hot cum I've had building in my balls since I met her into her waiting womb.

I *drench* the inside of her pussy with my seed. She takes it all as the orgasm flows through me, leaving a blissful wreckage in its wake.

After the last drop has left me and entered her, I collapse on the bed beside her with an exhausted groan.

We're both lying on the bed, staring at the ceiling as we try to catch our breaths. That was so intense. It was so fucking good.

The only thing I have left to do is to mark her, but I'm

not going to do that tonight, no matter how badly my bear wants it. She's been through enough tonight.

I'll get to it soon. I claimed her pussy and took her virginity. That's going to have to be enough for tonight.

My bear growls in disapproval.

Too bad, I tell him. *Her needs come first. Always.*

CHAPTER NINE

Lucy

I forgot how nice it is to wake up in a bed. These sheets are like heaven. This mattress is divine.

Dylan is sound asleep beside me, his huge body slowly moving up and down with every relaxed breath he takes.

I stretch out under the sheets and take a deep breath as I rest my head on this amazing pillow and watch his huge hulking back muscles. His shoulders are enormous and I love how his back is shaped like a giant V.

Memories of last night come flitting back… Dylan's massive body hovering over me… His immense weight pushing down on me… That huge delicious cock stretching me out in the best possible way.

I moan while thinking about it and the sound wakes him up. He stirs with a groan and then quickly turns around. His face is tight at first, but relaxes as soon as he sees me still lying here beside him.

"Good morning," he says in a deep groggy voice. I grin as he rubs his eyes and then runs his hand through his hair, making it even messier. He's so freaking cute. I can't even. "Did you sleep well?"

"I've been sleeping in a tube at the park behind a school," I say with a laugh. "So yeah. I slept well. This bed is amazing."

He looks upset and I curse myself out in my head for bringing up my homelessness. I know hearing about it kills him since it was so unsafe and I was so vulnerable out there on my own. He's so protective that it's making him upset to think of me in a position like that.

"That was my past," I say as I wrap my arm around his warm body. "I'm here with you now. Safe and happy." I kiss his shoulder and he turns around with heat in his eyes.

Oh yeah…

I spread my legs for him as he crawls on top of me.

What a fun way to wake up…

~

I'm grinning like an idiot as I walk into the kitchen in Dylan's massive shirt. It goes past my knees and the head hole is so large that my entire left shoulder is exposed.

He's got me so distracted that I wandered in here looking for something to drink and wasn't expecting to see anyone else.

I freeze as eight people stare at me in shock.

"Hello," I say awkwardly as I look around the huge kitchen. A few are eating breakfast at the table, a few at the island, and one big guy who is probably Dylan's brother is at the stove frying a crazy amount of eggs. "Dylan's in the shower."

They don't look too happy to see me.

"We met last night."

"At the auction?" the guy at the island with the bright blue eyes asks. He's frowning as he looks at me.

"Yeah. At the auction."

Two of the girls are staring at me with curiosity. When I look at them, they look away.

"He purchased you?" the girl with the blonde hair at the sink asks. She doesn't look away when I look at her.

"He had too," I say with a nervous nod.

"For how much?"

The guy at the table is shaking his head.

I must say… I was expecting a warmer reaction than this. On the drive home, Dylan told me that his brothers and their mates would be thrilled to meet me. They look pissed.

"Too much," I say with a nervous laugh. "I would have gone home with him for free."

One of the girl scoffs.

"Well, he is my mate…"

All eight of them jerk their heads up and stare at me in shock.

"What?" one of the guys asks. "Say that again."

"What? The mate part?"

"You're mates?"

I nod. "Yeah. We're mates. I knew it immediately when I saw him."

They all jump up and cheer. I gasp as they surround me and look at me with new eyes and excited smiles. This was the reaction I was hoping for.

"Welcome," the blonde says as she pulls me to the table. "Can I get you some orange juice, Dylan's mate?"

"How many eggs do you want?" the guy at the oven asks as he points the spatula at me. "Nine? Ten?"

"Ummm..."

"I love your hair," another girl says as she runs her fingers through it. "Who styled it?"

"Umm," I say as they all hover around me, talking at once.

"What's your name?" one of the guys asks. "Where are you from?"

"Has she been marked?" another one asks. They all look at my neck.

My hand flies up to the tingling spot under my ear as my cheeks start to blush.

This is very overwhelming. I've never been surrounded by so many people before and I've definitely never been the center of attention like this.

Dylan appears in the doorway and my heart soars when I see him. His hair is damp from the shower and he has a fresh pair of jeans and a T-shirt on. He looks incredible.

"I see you've all met my mate, Lucy."

They all leave me and engulf him in hugs, congratulations, and hard slaps on the back. They look thrilled for their brother.

I grin as I watch them, knowing I'm finally in a place I can call home.

"Are you sure you want to do this?" Dylan asks as he hesitates in the field. He's shirtless with the gorgeous mountains behind him.

"Absolutely," I say. "He saved my life."

Dylan frowns. "I think that was me, but whatever."

"It was both of you," I say with a laugh.

He takes a deep breath and then shrugs. "Fine. He'll never hurt you."

"I know he won't."

I watch with wide eyes as he unbuckles his belt, unbuttons his jeans, and pulls his pants down, taking his underwear along with it.

Holy… that massive thing is *always* surprising.

"Don't come closer than that," he warns. "Are you sure you want to—"

"Yes!"

He sighs. "Okay, grizzly bear coming in three, two…"

Dylan shakes and convulses violently. His teeth are gritted as his eyes turn a bright golden color.

"…one…"

I hold in a scream as a massive grizzly bear explodes out of the man I love.

"Whoa," I whisper as the bear lets out a deep huff of breath. His golden eyes find me and he comes walking over on those enormous paws.

I'm not even scared. My heartbeat is calm and steady as he approaches.

He looks so powerful with his giant shoulders and mighty jaw. Every few seconds, he lifts his snout and sniffs the air. His protective eyes never leave me.

"Hello," I whisper as he steps within touching distance. I run my hand over his brown fur and smile as he lets out a low happy rumble.

He buries his wet nose against my stomach, making me laugh as he nearly pushes me off my feet.

I think back to the nights sleeping in my car. The nights in the park all alone. I'll sleep fine from now on knowing this protective bear has my back.

"Thank you for saving me last night," I whisper in his ear as I hug his head, wrapping my arms around his thick neck.

After hanging out with my new friend for twenty minutes or so, Dylan comes back out.

"Welcome back," I say as I watch him grab his jeans and slide them back on.

"Were you scared?"

"No," I say with a shake of my head. "Not at all. He wouldn't hurt me."

"I know," he says as he pulls on his T-shirt, putting an end to the erotic show. "I've never seen him so calm."

"Really?"

"He's always been so difficult," he says with a heavy sigh. "Always busting my balls. Always making life unbearable."

"Why?"

"Because of you," he says with a shrug. "He couldn't rest until he was protecting his mate. Neither could I."

My heart is strumming as I step up to him. I gently touch his belt buckle as I lean in and kiss the bottom of his jaw. "I'm here now. You can both live in peace."

"I hope so," he says with a smile. "It feels nice."

He leans down and kisses me. I moan into his mouth and slide my arms around his neck. Fuck, he tastes good.

"What else do you want to do today?" he asks with a sexy smirk.

I just saw him naked, so I have all kinds of dirty things running through my mind that sound like a ton of fun.

But seeing his grizzly bear has brought out another urge in me. One that I can't quite shake.

"There is something I'd like to do," I tell him.

"Anything you want. Just let me know."

I sigh. "I'd like to find my dog."

CHAPTER TEN

Dylan

THIS IS NOT THE IMPRESSION I WANTED TO MAKE.

"Do you smell anything?" Lucy asks as she watches me sniff the corner of a brick building.

"Yeah," I say as I walk in the direction of Ziggy's scent. "I can smell him. He was here not too long ago. Probably this morning."

Smelling the street for a dog might not be the sexiest look I have, but Lucy looks so relieved that I suck up my pride and keep going.

"He went that way," I tell her when I catch his scent on the breeze.

"You can really smell him?" she says as she looks at me in amazement. "I can't smell anything."

"Most dogs can smell a hundred times better than a human can," I tell her. "A bloodhound can smell three hundred times better."

"Wow."

"My sense of smell, and any bear's for that matter, is seven times better than a bloodhound. Twenty-one hundred times better than a human."

"That's incredible," she says as she stares at me in awe. "Is there anything you can't do?"

"Scratch my back," I say with a laugh. "My biceps always get in the way."

She laughs as she walks over and scrapes her nails down my back, giving me shivers. "Good think you have me for that."

I'm about to kiss her when a fresh scent of Ziggy comes wafting over on the warm summer breeze. I snap my head in the direction of it.

"What is it?"

"He's close," I tell her before I start moving. She quickly follows me.

I run along the sidewalk in town and follow his scent into an alleyway behind a bakery. I've been tracking this mutt down for four hours. Lucy brought me to the spot where he was last seen when her car got stolen and I managed to pick up his scent after she found his favorite tennis ball in the gutter.

"This way," I say as the scent gets stronger and stronger. "He's around here for sure."

"Ziggy!" Lucy shouts when she turns the corner and sees him digging into a stale baguette.

He takes one look at her and starts wagging his tail so hard that his entire back half is shaking.

"Come here, boy!" she says as she kneels on the ground with her arms open wide. He drops the bread, sprints forward, and crashes into her so hard that she tumbles down laughing with him on top of her. I step forward as he licks her face.

Lucy told me he's a German Chow, which is a mix between a German Shepherd and a Chow Chow.

I can't believe the change in my bear. Normally he goes nuts around other animals, especially dogs. I'm used to him trying to burst out of me in a bloodthirsty rage, but he's as calm as can be while we watch our girl being lovingly reunited with her pet.

"I met your furry friend," Lucy says with a grin. "Come and meet mine. Dylan this is Ziggy. Ziggy this is Dylan."

I drop to a knee and pet the dog. He's wagging his tail as he smells me intensely. He's smelling my bear and curious about it.

"Thanks for keeping watch over our girl before I could," I say to him.

He licks my palm.

"Are you happy now?" I ask Lucy with a smile. "We have everything we need."

She touches the spot on her neck where my mark belongs. "Not everything," she says in a low voice. "It still feels like we're missing something."

I didn't want to mark her on the night I took her cherry. It would have been too much for her to handle.

But that's out of the way now and the urge to make her mine in that last final way is making itself known.

I'll mark her tonight.

And then, she'll be mine forever.

CHAPTER ELEVEN

Lucy

After walking Ziggy around the ranch outside, I set him up in the living room with a nice dog bed that Dylan was nice enough to buy him. He looks okay, but exhausted. I'd keep him in the bedroom with us, but I have a feeling that Dylan and I are going to keep him up all night long.

I'm already grinning as I bound up the steps and into our room.

"Dylan?" I say as I walk into the bedroom and look around. It's empty but the door to the bathroom is open a crack and the light is on.

The tiny hairs on the back of my neck stand up when I hear strange sounds that barely sound human—vicious snarling and growling.

"Dylan?" I whisper as I slowly walk across the room

toward the open door. Something falls over with a crash. A soap dish maybe? What the hell is going on in there?

I slowly push the door open and gasp when I see my man. He looks like he's mid-phase, just how he was when I first saw him at the auction house. Torn T-shirt and jeans, muscles swollen to double their normal size, teeth extended, eyes a shining golden color.

He turns away from me with a snarl. "Don't look," he says in a deep animalistic voice. "I don't want you to see me like this."

"You're my mate," I say as I slowly walk into the room. He's still turned away from me as I quietly close the door. "You don't have to hide from me."

He slowly turns back to me, his huge shoulders heaving up and down with every violent breath. His lips are pushed out from the long sharp canines that he's grown and he has long brown hairs growing out of the sides of his face. Long black claws are curving out of his fingertips. He looks like he's part monster, but I'm still attracted to him. I still think he's the most beautiful thing I've ever seen.

"What's wrong, baby?" I ask him softly. "You can tell me."

He grips the granite countertop so hard that a chunk of it snaps off in his big hand. "*Fuck,*" he growls as he tosses it on the floor. "It's my bear. He's not happy."

The spot under my ear starts tingling like never before. I touch it as I watch him struggling to control himself.

"Is it about the mark?" I ask, already knowing that it is.

"*Yes,*" he growls. "He won't fucking shut up about it."

My heart is pounding with nerves, but I want to do this. It's like the feeling before getting a tattoo, scared as hell for the needle, but excited for the final product.

"Mark me, Dylan," I say in a firm confident voice. "Give your bear what he wants. I'm ready for it. I'm ready to be yours in every way."

His golden eyes shine brighter as he looks at me. Suddenly his big strong hands are on me, turning me around and bending me over the sink. I whimper as he tears my pajama pants away. Rebecca lent them to me, but I can't worry about that now. I'll have to make it up to her some other time.

"I'll fuck you while I do it," he growls as my panties tear away with a hard yank of his hands. "It will help distract you from the pain."

It's distracting me alright. His big hard cock is pressing against my ass and it's all I can focus on.

He pulls down his jeans, grips his cock, and thrusts it into me with one hard pump of his hips. I cry out as I feel the full mighty size of him stretching out my pussy.

He's even thicker and longer than normal.

One strong hand grips my hip and the other grabs a fistful of my hair. I can feel the sharpness of his nails grazing me. I'm watching him through the mirror as he fucks me, that long thick dick sliding in and out with every hard thrust.

There's no romance this time. No holding back. He's fucking me hard like an animal, jerking me against the sink as my cries get louder and louder.

It feels so damn good. His cock is incredible.

I'm so focused on it, so focused on him through the mirror, that I don't notice him lunging toward my exposed neck before it's too late.

His teeth sink into my flesh with a growl. His long sharp canines pierce the spot that was destined for his mark.

I scream out as I feel him sucking my skin. His hand is gripping my hair, pulling my head back to keep my neck exposed. His big dick moves faster and harder.

"Oh shit," I moan as I feel an orgasm rushing forward. "Oh yes, Dylan. Fuck yes."

I cum hard all over his cock. His teeth slide out of my skin and he growls in my ear as he releases deep in my pussy.

The heat of his cum filling me and the intensity of my orgasm mixes with the blissful feeling of being marked by my mate. It's so overwhelming. It's so goddamn perfect.

I watch him through the mirror as my orgasm makes its way through my veins. His golden eyes turn back to their natural green, the long hairs on the sides of his face recede until they're gone, and I can feel the claws on his fingertips leaving and turning back into skin.

When he finally pulls out of me, we both collapse onto the bath mat. We're out of breath as we watch each other, not knowing what to say. It feels like we've just been through something special. Through something that will change everything.

I reach up and gently touch the mark. It feels like a pulsating heat, but it doesn't hurt. It feels good. Like the world finally makes sense. Like I'm right where I belong.

"I love you, Lucy," my man says as he looks at me with his green eyes overflowing with adoration.

I curl into his embrace and let him hold me. This man saved me in so many ways. He was right there when I needed him and I know he's never going to let me go. I'll never be alone again.

"I love you too," I whisper as he holds me tight.

I close my eyes and feel the heat of his mark, the

warmth of his love, and the wonderful feeling of being at peace in a place I can finally call home.

EPILOGUE

Lucy

Twenty years later…

"I'M FIRST!" MY YOUNGEST, BROCK, SHOUTS AS I WALK INTO the living room with a huge bowl of popcorn.

"I should be first," Melanie says. "I did the dishes!"

"I dried!" Connor replies.

All five of our kids are staring at the large bowl with their tongues hanging out. I quickly put it on the table before these little monsters jump me.

"Easy," Dylan says with a laugh as they all lunge on the bowl, popcorn flying everywhere.

"They get this from you," I say with a grin as we watch them wrestling and pushing each other as they all try to get the most popcorn into their clenched hands.

"I'm quite aware," Dylan says with a laugh as he puts

his feet on the table and looks at me with a loving smile. I'll never get sick of that look.

It's been twenty years together and I'm still so in love with this man.

We've had five kids and life has never been better.

Once all of the women around here started pumping out babies at an insane rate, the house got too small for all of us. It was fun living together and I miss those good old days, but eventually we all had to build our own houses on the ranch. We still use the original house for business and for family dinners on the weekends where we all squeeze in and always have a blast.

"I'm starting the movie," Dylan warns as he grabs the remote control.

The kids disperse from the empty bowl and squeeze onto the couches, the chairs, and whoever doesn't get a spot lays on the floor while the opening credits start to roll.

I'm too busy admiring the side of Dylan's face to pay any attention to the movie.

He has his big comforting arm around my shoulders and he pulls me a little closer as he does that little scrunching thing with his nose that I love so much.

I couldn't be happier.

Sometimes I think about the days when I was homeless and the best option I had going for me was letting myself be sold in a barbaric auction.

I've come a long way from there and it's all because of Dylan. He saved me in so many ways.

I don't even want to think about where I'd be without him.

Without my mate. My man. My dreamboat of a husband.

He looks down at me with a smile. "What is it?" he whispers.

"Nothing," I whisper shyly. "Just thinking about how much I love you."

He kisses me on the temple and holds me a little tighter. "I love you too."

My heart feels so full that sometimes it feels like it's going to burst.

This is one of those moments.

I'm so grateful for my kids and for my crazy grizzly bear mate.

Every day I'm thankful for that auction and for Dylan being my highest bidder.

Maybe he wasn't the highest bidder, but he was the growliest.

And I'm thankful for that too.

The End!

COME AND JOIN MY PRIVATE FACEBOOK GROUP!

Become an OTT Lover!

www.facebook.com/groups/OTTLovers

When I look out my office window and see her in the next building, I know I have to have her.

I buy the whole damn company she works for just to be near her.
She's going to be in my office working under me.
Under, over, sideways—we're going to be working together in *every* position.
This young innocent girl is going to find out that I work my employees *hard.*
And that her new rich CEO is already beyond *obsessed* with her.

This dominant and powerful CEO will have you begging for overtime! Is it just me or is there nothing better than a hot muscular alpha in a suit and tie!
All my books are SAFE with zero cheating and a guaranteed sweet HEA. Enjoy!

AUDIOBOOKS

Check out my complete collection of audiobooks at www.OliviaTTurner.com!

I'm adding more of your favorite OTT stories all the time!

DON'T BE SHY. COME FOLLOW ME...

I WON'T BITE UNLESS YOU ASK ME TO

Olivia T. Turner

www.OliviaTTurner.com

facebook.com/OliviaTTurnerAuthor
instagram.com/authoroliviatturner
goodreads.com/OliviaTTurner
amazon.com/author/oliviatturner
bookbub.com/authors/olivia-t-turner

Printed in Great Britain
by Amazon

25952451R00061